Hidden Tears
Still Marching

204
For Zee:
With much love!

Hidden Tears
Still Marching

A Civil War Story

By
Lindsey Guffrey

Hidden Tears Still Marching: A Civil War Story
ISBN: 978-0-88144-116-1

Published by
Yorkshire Publishing
9731 East 54th Street
Tulsa, OK 74146
www.yorkshirepublishing.com

In loving memory of my late stepfather, James P. Hogan, a well-known author who inspired me to finally publish my first short novel.

Contents

Author's Note

Looking back, I think of this story as one of many treasured mementos from my childhood. Originally written in March of 1995, when I was in eighth grade and not yet 14 years of age, it is finally finding its way to publication. From a handwritten document to being typed professionally, its original form has only been slightly altered to improve grammar and facts placed in this historical fiction story. However, most of it remains as originally written.

An interesting historical fact about the era in which the story took place is that the Emancipation Proclamation mandated by President Abraham Lincoln did not free the slaves in Northern border states such as Maryland. It only freed slaves in the Southern states. Many speculated that this was due to the fear that some of the border states that were still part of the North would have seceded, too, had they been required to immediately abolish slavery. As profound a leader as President Lincoln was, even he had his politics. Another important fact to note was that, during this time, Southern states had their own assumed president; Jefferson Davis.

As a combat veteran myself, I am able to reflect on this manuscript with interest. As a child, I was, in many respects, a "rebellious pacifist"; hence came the creation of a young protagonist still searching for meaning through journaling. Although I know now that wars can rarely be won through the use of non-violence alone, it is clear from the views of the two main characters—a teenage schoolboy and an escaped slave—that my priorities have always leaned towards violence only as an absolute last resort.

It is my hope that everyone who reads *Hidden Tears Still Marching: A Civil War Story* will also feel compelled to read my upcoming personal story about my own modern-day combat experiences, titled *Faith Beyond Fear: The Story of an American Soldier.* On this note, I would like to thank my family and friends for believing in me and my fans and supporters for making publication of this book possible. God bless and please enjoy.

Preface

From the journal of Private Daniel Samsford of the 18th Maryland

July 4th, 1863

I prayed before this month began that it would be better than the last. I believe now that I did not pray hard enough. We marched into the town of Gettysburg from Northern Virginia five days ago. I knew we were in for battle, but I didn't know that it would be this bloody. I thought that the Rebels would retreat or there would be none to fight. I read about the bloody battles before Billy and I volunteered. I thought whatever they gave me I could handle. Billy said we'd both regret it later if we didn't take part; of course, I believed him. I know now that's what killed him; he said he'd never go if I didn't come. I can't understand it. He was the soldier boy. I gave up my college scholarship to watch him get killed by the Rebel Army. He's only been dead for less than two days, but already I feel lost.

The only reason I didn't go crazy watching them soldiers die of the flu and fever, bronchitis, malaria, and pneumonia in the winter was because of Billy. It's because he was always there by my side that

I managed when I saw all of them with hacked off arms and legs. I survived when our regiment got spread with the measles, and I learned to accept the cut food shares they gave us. If it wasn't for him, the last six months would have been the worst half year imaginable.

Now that he's dead and our whole regiment is scattered, I don't know where to go. I don't know how many more days of this I can handle. I was able to find fifteen from my regiment; we're marching with some others down south until we find an officer to tell us where to go. We've been picking up strays along the way.

I don't think I'll ever be safe or happy again. I realize that war does no good for anyone. I think the bloodshed from the past three days has made me lose it. Billy shouldn't have died. It should have been me; it was a stupid thing for him to give his life for me. Because I gave up school and I ain't no farmer like he was, I'll always be good for nothing. Now I'm wandering the woods with a bunch of shook up men I hardly know, and none of us know where we're going. I heard General Meade said that we won the battle of Gettysburg, but any fight with that much bloodshed, I think there are no winners; we're all losers.

I want to go home or die, and don't give a damn which comes first anymore, as long as it gets me away from this hell on earth.

Chapter One

Billy was my big brother. I loved him more than anything else in the whole world. He always protected me and made me feel wanted and needed. Before going to war we were both so busy doing different things that we never had time to have a really close relationship, but even then I felt deeply for him. But it wasn't until New Year's Day of 1863 when we both together rebelled against our father and signed the contracts stating that we were devoted to serving two years in the Union Army that we were bound together forever. Until death do us part. I was only 16; a boy full of foolishness and excited for adventure. My brother, being 25 fought for much wiser reasons. After we enlisted we didn't talk much about why we were fighting. I figured he liked the excitement and triumph of victory like the rest of us. It wasn't until the last gasps of breath left him on the gruesome battlefield that I discovered the truth about my beloved brother. I tried to forget he'd said it.

How hard it is for me to tell about such a horrifying chapter of my life. But I know that I must speak about the hidden truth that I was then afraid to face.

For the first 16 years that I lived, all I had known was life in a school house. My mother tried to teach me to read and write at a very young age; she regretted giving up her first son to all farming and no schooling. She got sick with black water fever and died when I was five. Her father then handed my father a small fortune thinking that he needed it to finish raising up Billy and me. With that he could afford to send me to a nice boarding school that I went to until war came around. My father even bought himself a slave to help Billy and the farmers do the dirty work on his 52-acre farm. I remember some people saying what a cruel, sinning Christian my father was to go down south and buy himself our slave, Prem. But that was only because we lived in a small town called McSherville in southern Maryland. However, most people there didn't see one slave as much of a problem.

I only came home on weekends and holidays, but I knew that Billy disliked Father. He said he wanted to get rid of us and sometimes treated him as a slave. I understood him, for my same disliking for the man caused me to give up a scholarship to the University of Maryland. I only felt satisfaction for that decision after I became friends with Teddy Blocodle. However, my father having Prem never bothered me. I disliked Father for what he did to us, not to him. But I had no idea what Father did to him; I never helped with the farm so I rarely talked with Prem and had no relationship with him. I had learned about the slave trade in school but I never stopped to realize that I was prejudiced and Billy wasn't, until I met Teddy Blocodle.

Father truly did not want us fighting, especially for the North. That's much of why we did. When we joined the 18th Maryland, we were told we'd be in battle after no more than four months of marches and drills. But in all of March and part of April, our whole regiment got spread with the measles. Over a fifth of us died, and a sixth more from other diseases from January to July. Because of the measles, we weren't put into battle until Gettysburg.

After our regiment was killed and/or wounded, the few survivors along with other mixed regiments began to march south under the command of Major Vendgales. I would have marched right home from the battlefield, but Billy's death made my mind move slow. Also, marching with the other men made it difficult to run away.

So we marched in fear of rebel attack or ambush for days and miles of hot, open fields, and into dark, spooky forests. Finally, we reached Coal Fort ten miles west of Richmond. There we met up with General William Rosecrans and joined his Army of Cumberland, increasing its size greatly. I noticed that there were many black men in the Cumberland.

From Coal Fort, General Rosecrans began to march us further south for a reason I was not sure of and did not much care about. This is where my story begins.

Chapter Two

From the journal of Private Daniel Samsford of the 3rd Regiment in the Army of Cumberland.

July 21st, 1863

A lot has occurred since Independence Day. A lot of the boys are excited about it all, but I'm not one of them. I don't know what they did with Billy. They probably just stole his rifle and threw his body in a hole; I don't care.

There is no longer an 18th Maryland; I'm now under the command of General William Rosecrans and his Army of Cumberland. We already marched through Maryland. Now we're in southern Virginia marching for the Tennessee river, near the Georgia line; close to some small town called Chattanooga that we're trying to claim. If you ask me I just think this land claiming ain't worth much when you kill all of the people who were planning to own it. We ain't marching fast enough, though; officers say the Rebels will be expecting us since we won a lot of battles. Also, if we march slowly, we get fewer food shortages. This is because the longer we stay close to a centralized location the more shipments we are able to receive. That means more to eat.

The reason that there's so much excitement that I can't relate to is because everyone thinks that we're surely going to win the war. But I think that we're all going to die first. When there isn't anything that a good-for-nothing private like myself can do to change it, why the hell should I give a damn? Even if I could go home now, my father would not forgive me. I believe he is losing his farm without Billy working and with Prem running away. My father said in a letter I got a month ago that he thinks that Prem joined a black Yankee regiment. That was the only letter that he sent me.

The siege of Vicksburg was won on Independence Day; I heard we finally got the Mississippi River now. I also heard General Banks won us Port Hudson down in Louisiana on the 9th. Everyone thinks God smiled on us because we won three sieges and fights in the same week. I think that the devil struck us. How the hell can we be victorious with three battlefields full of bodies and blood?

I want to take whatever comes up, get it over with, and move on. I know I'll fear some of it, but I also know that it has to end sometime. Maybe I won't live to see it end, but at least I won't know that I'm dead.

Chapter Three

That was the way I thought for a while without Billy around. I didn't talk to too many people; I was shy and didn't want to get friendly with anyone else. I would have never admitted it then, but I know now that I feared having a friend. I knew that I'd have to suffer losing him, too.

However, I always tried to act tough around the other guys, like I could take anything. I made it look like I enjoyed being a loner, as if I didn't enjoy anyone or anything. I suppose most of them bought it, because when I joined the 3rd Cumberland I was separated from all who had known Billy.

That was until the tenth of August, when I met a man who could see clear through me. It was more than a month after I had become lost forever, but he helped me change my ways. I admit with much regret that I wouldn't have chosen him as a guide or even a friend if I had had the choice. I doubt any white boy of my years, who had lived with a slave and had seen such sick sacrifices, would have done so in the middle of a civil war.

No matter what, you can't change the past; but I would never want to change my short lasting friendship with Teddy Blocodle. I only would have changed my ignorance and uneducated assumptions toward his kind.

Chapter Four

From the journal of Private Daniel Samsford of the 3rd Regiment in the Army of Cumberland.

July 30th, 1863

We're in northeastern Tennessee right now; we marched to the border three days back and set up camp there. All of the officers were discussing military strategy. They're telling us they have it all figured out; how we're going to take Chattanooga, I mean. They say this battle may end the war and lead us to victory against the Rebs. I seem to be the only one without the confidence and belief to lead us to victory. I think the generals are trying to make us want to fight by filling our heads with lies about the thrill of victory.

I saw General Rosecrans last night. He talked to our regiment and all the others of Cumberland; I don't know how many there are of the men who will join us when we get to base camp. He said they're marching up from Port Hudson and they all fought there. They all got separated like us Gettysburg fighters, but I hear a plenty of them are gonna be joining us. He said we need lots of men for this battle because it will be extremely important, and it will be better as a siege. I no longer understand how people can want to plan a battle and create a bloodbath.

He also says that there is still no rush. When we do get to base camp in about a week, we'll wait, make more attack plans, and get word from General Grant and President Lincoln before the siege and attack. This whole idea of slowly planning our kill is really disgusting me.

Because our regiments are so small (ours is only 515 men and five commanding officers), the men from Port Hudson are going to be put into the regiments of Cumberland instead of making more. Less than a month after I fought the bloodiest battle of this war so far, these rich generals are already planning our next sick battle!

I wonder if any of the men joining our regiment from Port Hudson will be civilized enough to realize that a country fighting and killing itself is wrong. I doubt it.

Chapter Five

At 16 I thought I knew everything. Because I had been in school for over ten years, I even thought I was too smart for college. But when it came to the outside world, I knew nothing. That was the truth. My mind was inside Billy's. I did not have a mind without him. I felt and even knew that I would have been better off dead. However, I did not regret anything. I was way too angry to regret. Angry with war, angry with the Rebs, angry with the Yanks, angry with the generals, angry with Lincoln, and angry with Gettysburg. Everything that had anything to do with Billy's death made me angry. I was even angry with myself, and at him.

But one man who I thought I was angry with helped me overcome all of my anger and unnecessary hatred. I knew him for little more than a month of my life.

Chapter Six

From the journal of Private Daniel Samsford of the 3rd Cumberland.

August 6th, 1863

We arrived at base camp headquarters this morning. We're quite near the Tennessee River. Standing on a high point, you can easily spot it and much of Georgia beyond. When we got here, many tents were already set up and the soldiers from Port Hudson were waiting for us.

They divided the men up into regiments. They put exactly 220 new men in our regiment, ten of whom are black. This made many of the soldiers furious, having Negroes in our regiment; they all think we should throw them out. I agree with them. Sleeping in the same tent as a black man or sharing the same clothes or even simply being in one of the same regiments can make many feel uncomfortable. How can you know if one of them won't rob one of us in the night? They could steal our things or slit our throats if all comes to worst. My pa said they been known to do things like that, and he's an expert when it comes to Negroes; he had one. Although Prem never did any harm to anyone that I can remember. Billy said he was a great guy.

However, I think Billy may have been lying because Prem did escape. But still, I know those Negroes have never been educated and they shouldn't put them with us. Our Lieutenant Colonel told us that Rosecrans directly ordered it that way. He must be crazy! He said it was because so many were killed at Port Hudson. There ain't enough to make their own black regiment, so they had to mix them all with us. From what I heard, after Chattanooga they're gonna fix it all up and get them separated from us. That made some feel more secure, but I still think they should stick them somewhere else now, and I'm definitely not the only one.

However, it ain't gonna get to me as much as some of the others because I ain't got nothing to lose. If a Negro slits my throat as long as I don't know it was him, I won't give a damn. I wonder what Billy would have thought; his ways were weird. I know if I had to share a tent with one I'd probably care more. I wouldn't want their smell on me. I hear they smell really bad.

But as long as they don't kill any of us Yanks, I'm not gonna make any protests. They better leave me be, like everyone else. I know we're gonna be stuck with them for at least a month, then we're gonna have to fight in the same bloody battle as them, on the same side. I suppose since I can't change any of it; being a Private and all, I have to live with it until I die. Billy would probably think the same way. I've forgotten what he looks like, but I think his eyes were hazel.

Chapter Seven

Four days after I wrote that entry I met someone who would completely change the way I thought. I was wandering through the forest looking for a comfortable spot to digest. It was around noon; we had finished our long drills and practice marches. I picked a spot behind a large oak tree and began my business. All of a sudden I felt something strong and brutal strike my head, and I crashed to the ground, nearly unconscious.

I then felt someone unlacing my boots. I heard a loud huffing noise that the person appeared to be making. He seemed to be fearing something, but I couldn't bring myself to open my eyes. Then I felt him undoing my leather belt. I began to twitch my eyes, trying very hard to open them. I then heard him pull my carving knife out of its belt pouch. My eyes flung open. There I saw a crazy looking black man with several small bald spots, rotted teeth and dirty, torn clothes holding a knife tip down, directly above my neck. My eyes widened. I couldn't move. I thought I was dead for sure.

He was about to bring the knife down on my neck when a large, dirty black hand grabbed his head and yanked him away. I backed off as quickly as I could, and sat upright, catching a glimpse at what was happening. The bigger black man threw the knife out of the crazy one's hand. He also grabbed the boots and leather belt and threw them in my direction. I glanced over at them but did not pick them up. I listened to the larger Negro speak to the crazy one.

"Now listen here, friend. I know you're scared, but he ain't after you. He don't want to kill you and neither do I, so don't make things worse than they have to be. We'll let you go on about your business if you let us go on about ours. Work for you?" He asked this with no tremble of fear as he stuck out his hand calmly.

The crazy man looked at the mellow, large one as he squinted his eyes. He stared at him for a few moments as the fear in his eyes began to fade. He then shook his hand and began running further into the woods. The other black man stood still and watched him leave. Then he walked to where he threw my carving knife and picked it up. He walked over to me, picked up my belt and put the knife in its pouch. He held the belt out in front of me. I grabbed it away quickly and began to strap it around my waist. I was a little embarrassed to discover that my pants were still down, so I quickly pulled them up without hesitation. The black man didn't seem to mind.

"Are you all right?" he asked looking directly in my eyes.

"Who the hell was that?" I scowled furiously. "He almost killed me! You should have let me slit the bastard's throat!"

"He didn't know what he was doing."

"How do you know that?" I questioned him.

"Because I seen his kind before. That man there was an escaped slave running from his masters. He must have thought you were one of the slave hunters."

"Well, don't he know what a blue uniform on a white man means?" My voice rudely hissed as I held up my head.

"Apparently not, sir. He was probably looking for free land, fearing anything else that moved."

"You should have let me kill him!" I stared at the tall, muscular black man.

"Sir, I ain't one to make such a decision to end the life of a helpless, scared man. Besides, the slave catchers most likely gonna catch him soon anyway; he didn't know where he was going." The man showed attempted politeness in his voice.

"You just didn't want him dead because you're both Negro brothers, right?" I spoke with certainty.

The man just looked at me with his shiny black eyes. I could see his curved chin, scuffed up cheeks and roughly-grown, dirty, short, dark hair.

"I believe all men are brothers, not just black or white men. I would have done the same if it were you trying to kill him."

I looked at him in confusion. The small lines and cracks near his eyes and jaw proved him to be around thirty.

"It wouldn't have been me trying to kill him, and why were you here anyway? Were you spying on me?"

"Oh no sir, not at all. It was my duty assigned by Major Prehan that I hand out lunch for our section of the regiment, every day that there is one. You was gone so I went looking for you. We're in the same regiment, you know." He held out a wrapped cloth. I grabbed it, stood up and peeked inside to see a piece of hardtac and a red apple. "Just got a new shipment of fruit; the apples are fresh," he kindly mumbled. "My name's Teddy Blocodle. What's yours?" He stuck his hand out and showed his crooked smile.

I did not shake. I did not want to touch his grubby, black hand. I simply said, "Daniel Samsford," and laced my boots.

"Samsford, where have I heard that name before?" Teddy questioned his own mind. "Well, I suppose it will come to me."

"Teddy, if that's your real name, I'm going back to base now. I need to check up before they presume me dead."

"Yes, I should check up also. Major Prehan must be wondering about me."

We began to walk back. I tried to run ahead, but the dizziness in my head prevented me from doing so. When we arrived back at base, we had a somewhat rare midday three-hour break. I took advantage of this occasion by sleeping off my headache the whole time inside my sleeping bag in our four-person tent, before waking up and practicing drills and marches the rest of the day. I don't know what Teddy did for our break; probably cleaned up and took orders.

That night I began thinking about what had happened. I also thought about one of the things Billy had said. I know he said a lot of things, most of which made no sense, but I still tried to figure them out. He said, "Pride ain't something you should be proud of. It's something that others give you without you knowing it. But courage is different; it's something that you have to find on your own. It takes even a little bit of courage to accept and appreciate others, and it takes even more to realize that you'll never be better than anyone else."

Those were Billy's words. He didn't ever feel like he had to impress anyone. He didn't think that the Rebels were the enemy; he thought of them as an obstacle. "In order to reach peace, we must go through them," he had once said. He also said he knew that the Rebs were just like us, but if he dwelled on that, he'd never get the nerve to fight and kill them.

This was the first time I'd thought about Billy since his death. I had almost completely forgotten about our good times, and it made me feel peculiar thinking about him. I knew it was Teddy's actions that made me remember. I even remembered what he looked like. His foresty green eyes, his long, rugged brown hair, and his scruffy face. The way his chin and cheek bones curved and flattened like mine, and the way his nose was round like mine, except a little bit longer. I smiled in the presence of my thoughts, trying to seize what I would soon forget and soon regret.

I had to talk to Teddy again. I didn't have to be friends with him, I just had to thank him for saving my life. I knew Billy would have made me.

Chapter Eight

Daniel Samsford, 3rd Cumberland,
Fort Millgrow Base

August 10th, 1863

Today was a confusing day. The first three days that we were here were normal. Plenty of practice drills and marches; Colonel Subir gave us this long lecture yesterday about medical care. He said that two miles uphill there is a medical camp with plenty of trained doctors, and we should go there for all injuries. Afterwards, all of the privates agreed that the doctors are killers. I know they'd have to tie me up and drag me there before I got treatment from them.

Today I got a head injury that I can still feel. But I didn't see no doctors; they would have hacked off my head. Instead I got lots of rest. The way I got the injury is quite confusing. I was digesting yesterday's dinner when some hard rock or stick hit my head. Some black slave was trying to rob me; he almost killed me with my own knife. Then another Negro grabbed him away from me and said some stuff to him; trying to talk him out of killing me, I guess. It worked. The man who saved me said his name was Teddy Blocodle; he gave me my stuff back. I didn't thank him; he looked like a dirty Negro, but now I think I should. He must have saved my life.

I know that because of him, I even remember what Billy looks like, and some of the weird things he said. He's in my regiment so if I see him tomorrow, I'll tell him I appreciate what he did, but I won't get too friendly with him. That might be too dangerous. I remembered today that Billy's eyes were forest green. I won't forget again.

Chapter Nine

We awakened the next morning at five, our usual time, and we entered directly into the day. Getting set into uniform, I ate my juicy apple from the day before. We did some boring practice drills, and marched 12 practice miles, listened to the officers tell us about seige attack plans and did some more drills. Finally it was lunch break.

For lunch all we received was a dried piece of hardtac. But I suppose that is better than many days when we didn't even have a lunch, or even worse a full day with no food at all. We were all lined up straight, receiving our share, as I saw Teddy passing the bread in a large cloth bag. One man about ten persons down from me refused to accept anything from a "damn Negro". The soldier next to him took two pieces.

When Teddy got around to me, I held out my hand. He gently placed a piece of hardtac in it. My chapped mouth opened, but no words came out. Teddy looked directly into my round, sky-blue eyes as I brushed back my dry, tangled, dirty blonde hair.

"You go ahead and take my piece as well, Mr. Samsford," he set another square of bread in my hand. "I ain't never been one for solid bread anyway."

I left my hand out and mouth open as Teddy continued to pass out bread. After a few moments passed, my mouth finally mumbled a word. "Teddy?"

"Yes, sir?" We once again made direct eye contact, from about ten feet.

I paused for a moment longer. "Thank you for your kindness."

He simply nodded in my direction and replied, "Thank you for yours, young boss," and he continued his duty.

Teddy's few words of that conversation did not make me feel any better. I knew I was not even the least bit kind to him. I had cursed him after he had saved me from a knife in the throat, and I had just stolen his lunch. Although I did not regret my rudeness, I still felt I shouldn't be given credit for something that I did not do.

He, on the other hand, had given me more kindness than all the other men in our regiment and asked for nothing in return. That was what he got from everyone: nothing.

I did not know what to think of it or what to say to Teddy next. So I let him do his job and tried to relax, waiting for our next drill.

That night was quite cold for August. We could not build a fire inside our tent because there was barely enough room for the four of us to lay down comfortably as it was. Also, the smoke inside an enclosed tent would not be too safe. So I crawled outside catching a breath of crisp, cold, fresh air. While wrapping my sleeping bag around my arms in an attempt to stay warm, I spotted a fire off in the distance. It was three rows in front and nine tents down from the one where I was sleeping. I stood up to catch a better glimpse. Because of my shortened night vision I could not make out who the men were. Nonetheless, I began to slowly walk towards them.

I heard a unique, rhythmic sound coming from some strange instrument I had not heard before. One of the men by the fire was playing it. I began to walk over there more quickly to see what was happening.

I suddenly stopped directly in front of the fire. It was Teddy playing the instrument; he and three other black men were circled around the fire. I stood there listening to him play his soul-touching melody. I was a bit afraid and embarassed to approach any closer. The instrument was no bigger than the palm of his hand.

After finishing the song, which I had never heard anything like before, Teddy looked up at me. "You look cold," he said. "Why don't you come sit by our fire and warm yourself up?"

I looked down at the men, they were all smiling and looked welcoming enough. "Okay," I mumbled quietly.

Teddy scooted to the right giving me a pleasable spot to sit by the fire. I was warmed up in seconds and began to feel more comfortable. I still had my sleeping bag wrapped around me. "Guys, this is Sir Daniel Samsford," Teddy pointed in my direction. "Daniel, this is Shawn next to me, this here is Jim, and that's Walt."

"Pleased to meet you," Jim smiled.

"It's quite a pleasure," said Walt.

"Nice meetin' ya," Shawn spoke.

"Hi," I shyly mumbled looking at their dark faces. "What was that thing you were playing that unusual song on?" I questioned Teddy.

"Well, we call that soul music and this is a harmonica." Teddy held up the small, silver instrument.

"How'd you learn to play it?" I wondered. There was a long pause after my question.

"A friend of mine gave it to me before he was killed."

"Did he die at Port Hudson?"

"No," Teddy replied firmly. "My master in Virginia shot him."

I quickly jumped to my feet in shock. "You're an escaped slave aren't you?!" I shouted with anger. "How could I have been fooled by a black man?"

Teddy calmly looked straight at me. "Yes, Daniel, I am. But I only escaped to help free all the slaves and help all the people. My master was teaching hatred, and no love. I ain't trying to hurt no one. Please, sir, try to accept me as a person."

I looked deeply at the profound Negro man with great misunderstanding. But still I attempted to piece the information together. I slowly, nervously stepped toward the empty spot by the fire next to

Teddy. Why was I approaching him again? Why did I not run back to my tent? They wouldn't have followed. Why did I want to stay here with an ugly ex-slave? I wasn't sure, but I felt it was something about his way with words. His words were difficult to follow; they were similar to Billy's.

Teddy Blocodle had a strange, unique, certain glimmer of honesty in his eye. So I once again sat down next to him and asked him another question. "If you're not trying to hurt anyone, then how come you're killing Rebs?"

"Well, I ain't," he replied.

"What do you mean?"

"I mean I ain't killed any Confederates. I actually ain't killed no one."

"But you fought at Port Hudson. Did you miss every time you shot?" I was confused.

"I ain't ever even tried to kill no one, or even fight with them. While the battle was going on I fired my gun in the sky a few times, but never where it would hit anyone, sir."

"Well, why the hell are you in a war if you ain't gonna kill anyone? What good does that do?" I scowled.

"What good does killing people do, sir? It just causes more killing and more tears. I came here to help people, like you; plus I had nowhere else to go. Daniel, I will accept your ways if you will accept mine," Teddy quietly whispered.

Then he pulled out a Bible from his inside pocket and held it up. "My Daddy gave this to me when I was a boy. I ain't never been able to read a single word in it, and neither could my Daddy. I ain't never been to church, but I learned from somewhere that one of the Ten Commandments from the Lord is to never kill. I've always remembered that and have yet to go against it." Teddy gently placed the Bible back in his pocket and looked into my eyes with that gleam of honesty still in his. "I ain't never even been in a fist fight with another man; unless I meet eyes with something that's truly worth fighting for, I don't plan on doing so."

"What's truly worth fighting for?" I asked.

"A friend," he answered simply.

"What about the friend your master killed? Why didn't you fight for him?"

"I tried Daniel, I truly did, but the white man got the gun." I saw a small tear fall from Teddy's eye.

I looked at him more closely. "Now you got the gun Teddy, and you ain't even willing to use it."

He held his head up higher and looked in my direction. "I ain't like my old master, sir. Now I know that you ain't either, but if I shoot a man, I'll be just as bad as him."

There was no arguing with that. The man was right; we must respect each other's ways. Billy probably would have said the same damn thing. "You don't have to call me 'sir,'" I informed him. "I'm younger than you are."

He looked up at me and gave a half grin. "Okay Daniel, I won't call you 'sir' anymore."

I nodded at him to show a little appreciation. Jim, Walt, and Shawn appeared to be having their own conversation, paying no attention to ours.

"Daniel?"

"Yes, Teddy?"

"Remember yesterday when you introduced yourself to me?"

I lowered my head slightly, believing that he would recall my rude behavior. "Yes," I answered.

"Well, remember how I mentioned that I heard your last name somewhere before?"

I looked up again; I was curious about what he was getting at. "I think so," I replied.

Now Teddy looked up at me. "I remembered this morning where I had heard it," he said.

"Where?" I anxiously asked.

"When we was camping in the trenches we dug at Port Hudson, we would talk to just about everybody, being pretty bored and all."

I opened my ears to Teddy's words as he continued to speak.

"On one of the days in late May when the siege had started, I met a black man from Maryland. I started talking to him because that's where I ran off to when I escaped. He said he'd run off from his master and joined the Union Army less than a month before." Teddy paused momentarily, then spoke again. "He told me about how he was the only slave on a small, 52-acre farm in McSherville, Maryland, and about how his master's two sons had joined the Union Army on New Year's Day. He said his master's name was George Samsford."

Upon hearing that I looked up at the dark sky and closed my eyes. "What did he say about my father?" I asked.

Teddy didn't hesitate to answer, but replied in a slow, detailed tone. "He said that after you boys ran off to war, your pa was working him extra hard, but his farm was still falling apart." He took a deep breath. "He told me that your pa started going crazy and he was angry all the time. He said that he was constantly whipping him and he almost killed him, and that's why he ran away. He didn't know anything that happened after he left." Teddy threw another stick in the fire.

"Where is he now?" I asked. "Did he stay down in Louisiana after you won the siege?" There was a long pause as I waited for the answer.

"No, Daniel, he was killed during our first pursuit," he gently whispered.

I closed my eyes once more and bit my lip.

"It was in late May," Teddy informed me. "General Banks sent out twenty-five hundred men to test the Confederate combat strength. It was mostly blacks he sent out; I guess because he saw us as the most expendable. I was one that got sent out, and so was your pa's slave. Two thousand of us was killed that day, he was one of them. The only reason I wasn't killed too was because I retreated in time; I was lucky." Teddy looked down and shook his head. "Poor old fool never even told me his name."

"Prem," I mumbled under my breath. "His name was Prem."

"I will remember that Daniel," he responded.

I then took a deep sigh and shook my head in confusion. "I guess old Prem really messed up, huh? He fears death from my pa so he risks so much trying to escape, only to be killed less than a month later."

"He did say that he liked his master's two sons," Teddy acknowledged.

"Did he?"

"Yeah, he said that the younger boy was quite the student. He told me that he rarely got to see you, but he always looked forward to the times that he did see you. He also said that he liked your brother a lot; Billy I think he said his name was. He said that he never yelled at or scolded him and that he was the farmer. He said that your brother didn't believe in slavery, and every time your pa made him do dirty work, that Billy would do it right along with him, to let him know that there were people who cared about him," Teddy looked at my pale cheeks. "Where is your brother now?"

I peered down at the fire and then raised my chin again. "Gettysburg," I answered. "He was shot in the chest by a Rebel bullet on the third day. I was standing right next to him."

"I'm very sorry," Teddy said kindly.

"So was I."

"Things happen in war, Daniel, sad things. We lose people we love. But you must remember that you are still alive. You can cry for the people you love, but eventually you have to hide your tears and keep on marching."

Upon hearing those words my eyes squinted at Teddy. Was he a mind reader? Weren't those Billy's words? "Hey, my brother—" I hesitated to finish. I remembered that I had almost completely forgotten about Billy's last words; I had tried to forget.

"What Daniel?" Teddy questioned. "What did your brother say?"

"Nothing," I retorted. I then pretended to yawn and attempted to change the subject. "I like that harmonica thing you were playing," I said. "That soul noise it makes is different. I love it."

Teddy pulled the handy instrument from his pocket. "Thank you," he said. "I like it also; perhaps I could teach you how to play it sometime." He stuck it back in his blue uniform, picked up a stick, and rearranged the firewood with it for a while.

After the passing of what seemed like a few long moments, he spoke in his soft, comforting voice again. "It's okay, Daniel," he said. "He was your brother, and I know how painful it can be to lose a brother. My older brother was sold to a man in Alabama 14 years ago when I was only 17. I never heard from him again after that, but I did not forget him. I know that it will hurt to remember, but I assure you that it will hurt even worse if you forget."

I brushed my light hair back and licked my lips, looking around the circle. Walt, Jim, and Shawn were still silent but appeared to be paying full attention to our conversation now. "On the battlefield when Billy was hit—" I paused momentarily. "I held him in my arms; he only had a few gasps of life left in him, and he used them as best he could.

He said to me, 'Don't worry Daniel, you were worth dying for; the hidden tears are still marching.' Then he was gone." I swallowed and wiped a small tear from my eye.

Teddy put his left hand on my shoulder and patted it. Later I was quite amazed that I did not even think about brushing it away. But it was something about his caring heart that kept me by the fire and pushed the truth out of me. "Do you know what he meant?" he asked me.

"He meant that every man deserved a tear from another man," I responded. "He also meant that when any man, woman, or child that you know dies, the least you can do is give them a tear. You should also be willing to shed a tear to save that person's life. He told me this earlier. He said that because so many people you know die in war, its hard to shed a tear for each one of them, so the tears remain hidden, but they still keep on marching inside the heart." I quoted my late brother as I brushed another tear from my eye. "But my tears for Billy are no longer hidden," I said as I looked over at Teddy. "You made me let them out."

Teddy nodded his head with satisfaction. "Do you agree with him?" he asked. "Would you be willing to cry for the death of any person you knew? And would you be willing to cry to keep any man you know alive?"

I straightened my posture for more comfort before answering. "Not any man I know," I said. "The man would have to prove himself worthy of my tears first."

"And how would he do that?" asked Teddy.

I paused for a moment to think of an answer. "I guess by doing something that would prove he'd shed the same tears for me."

"Real good answer, brother," Walt finally spoke with enthusiasm.

I gave a half smile as I stood up. "Thank you all for letting me warm by your fire."

"No problem," Jim gestured.

"I should get some sleep now," I said. "This five o'clock in the morning stuff gets to me."

"You come warm by our fire any night you want to," Shawn welcomed me.

"Good night, everybody," I began to head toward my tent.

"Daniel," Teddy's voice echoed as I glanced back around. "You're a good man," he proclaimed.

I nodded with shyness. “Same to you,” I mumbled before turning around and running towards my tent without looking back. When I arrived at my side of the campsite I stopped and began to wonder why I was running. How was a 30-year-old, illiterate black man making me remember how much I loved Billy? What was making me tell him all of the things that I thought I feared? Why was I beginning to feel that Teddy Blocodle, a man whom 48 hours ago I had never laid eyes on before in my life, was my new best friend?

It was all too confusing for me to think about at such a late hour at night, so I murmured to myself, “Damn, I must be going crazy.” Then I shook my head and smiled as I ducked in to my tent, crawled in to my sleeping bag, and went to sleep.

Chapter Ten

The next morning the sun was blazing right into my temporarily blinded eyes as I awoke. I quickly turned my head in the opposite direction to block its brightness; it was no longer cold. At first I was quite surprised at the thought of the sun being out before five o'clock in the morning, but then I remembered that it was Sunday. On most normal Sundays we had the privilege of sleeping in until six before doing practice drills and marches for the day. But we usually didn't have to work anywhere near as hard on Sundays as we did during the other six days of the week.

I sat up in my sleeping bag as I tried to recall all of the things that Teddy and I had talked about the night before. I was beginning to figure out why I had spoken to him. I remembered how I was angry with anyone or anything who was involved in making battlefields into blood baths, but he wasn't entirely involved. I knew he was a little involved because he was a soldier, but he was less involved than me. He'd never even tried to shoot any rebels, and I know that after they killed Billy I tried to shoot every one of them. I respected Teddy's ways, but I knew that if there were any more like him, the war would never end, and when it finally did, the Confederates would have victory.

In the presence of thinking these thoughts, knowing that at any moment the Lieutenant Colonel would fire his rifle for wake-up call, I suddenly heard the most heart-warming sound I had ever heard in my life. It was the sound of voices singing a beautiful song. It was like an opera, so well-set and arranged, I could feel the voices touching my soul. I stumbled out of my sleeping bag, threw on the coat and boots of my Yankee uniform, and trotted out of my tent.

I turned around and looked directly behind me. There I saw, at about 50 feet in distance, Teddy, Walt, Jim, Shawn, and two other black men sitting on a large rock, letting out all the beauty from their voices. They were singing "We Are Climbing Jacob's Ladder," a song I had heard once in my Catholic church, but I had never heard it being sung as extraordinarily as this.

"We are, we are climbing, climbing Jacob's ladder; soldiers, soldiers of the cross," Teddy chanted in lead as the others echoed.

As I glanced up at Teddy's spirited face, I could tell that he was looking straight at me. A tear fell from his partly bearded cheek, and I knew that he meant for the tear to be for me. He was singing for me, the whole song, all the people, everything; it was all for me. So I brushed the falling tears from my smooth face and soft cheeks as I closed my eyes. I tried to seize the incredibly beautiful moment I knew would shortly come to an end as I listened wholeheartedly to the words.

"Keep on, keep on, climbing, climbing, we will, we will surely make it, soldiers of the cross."

In hearing Teddy Blocodle sing me those last words to that extravagant song, I felt a burst of compassion for the man explode inside of me. I had rarely felt such compassion for another person. Right then I put my whole past behind me and my whole future ahead of me. All I could hear was the vibration of the song echoing within my soul, and all I could feel was the genuine compassion that was now being released from my heart. As of right then, I did not care what others said. I did not care how many people laughed at me and joked about me, or what they thought about me. At that moment I knew that Teddy Blocodle was my new big brother. Moreover, I knew that it was going to stay that way no matter what happened; just like with Billy, we would always be brothers.

So when Teddy stepped down from the rock, I ran straight into his arms and wept on his shoulder. From that point onward, every time I looked at another person's skin, I became color-blind.

I gently grasped the Holy Bible Teddy was holding and opened to Genesis, beginning with the story of Jacob and his 12 sons. I had been to church many times and had nearly the entire first book of Old Testament scripture memorized. So my new brother listened to the story in great detail, hearing the words of the Bible for the first time.

After that, between drills and marches, Teddy and I spent all of our spare time together, for the whole rest of the month of August. I read more scripture to him from his Bible, we baked bread over the fire, explored the woods together, went picketing together, and told stories together. We asked each other questions, told about our past, and spoke about our feelings around the fire. I asked him how Prem got to Louisiana so fast from Maryland, and he told me a little about the secret underground railroad that ran across the entire country, from north to south, and about the wonderful transportation of steam-powered trains. Teddy also asked me about my opinions on the war, and how I try to solve conflicts. I told him about my school years, and about my mother and father, and about how war actually brought my late brother and me closer together.

Teddy also told me about how the woman he was going to marry was sold out of state one week before their wedding date, and about how I was now the only one he had left to confide in about his true feelings. I told him that I felt the same way about him. He even taught me how to play his harmonica, and I continued to read him stories from the Bible at night. I was no longer lost or alone; I had a new friend and a new brother. My ways of thinking had been completely changed, for the better, forever, and I knew I owed it all to that one man.

Chapter Eleven

Private Daniel Samsford, 3rd Cumberland,
Fort Millgrow, Tennessee

August 19th, 1863

Since the last time I wrote I have had the most incredible experience of my life. The man who saved me from the escaped slave has become my new brother. He has proved himself worthy of all good things I could give him. He has helped me see the truth about war, about peace, about love, and about Billy. His ways are incredible, and although he is in this war and he has never been to church, he believes in the Bible, which I have been loyally reading to him. That is why he will not kill another man. He did not even try when he fought at Port Hudson. I admire his truthful willpower for that.

I have known Teddy for less than two weeks, but already we have told each other everything there is to tell about one another. I know many people must be talking about and laughing at me, but they have not gotten to me or him in the least, because they know nothing about color-blind love.

Unfortunately, my white tentmates have been harassing me about my newfound friendship. Others have been making fun of me as well, as if it's any of their business. They just don't know Teddy or the other black men in our regiment, and their attitudes have just motivated me to spend as little time as possible with them, and more time with Teddy and his other friends. Generally, I just try to ignore the rudeness from other young, white soldiers like myself. Most of them just aren't mature enough or decent enough individuals to have even a hint of compassion for others who are the least bit different. I see it as their loss, though.

Teddy is an extraordinary singer. His songs reach out and touch the depths of my soul, and the first one he sung to me is what bound us as brothers. He also has a little instrument called a harmonica that he can play wonderfully. Because of him, I am no longer angry with anyone. I believe Billy is with the Lord now, and they're both watching over me. I also believe now that all men are created equal, and I no longer have a wish for death, of any sort. Teddy has helped me be strong, accept myself and others, and face my fears. I am not afraid to show my true feelings or cry in front of him, and he is not afraid to do the same in front of me.

My grandpa once told me that war changes everyone and everything that has a part in it. However, he never said if it was for better or worse. For me, because a miracle has struck in my direction, I know it's for the better.

Chapter Twelve

Private Samsford, 3rd Cumberland,
Fort Millgrow, Tennessee

August 27th, 1863

Today was a fun day, but it was also exhausting. We woke up at four o'clock in the morning to get an early start on drills. We marched 17 practice miles today before coming back to camp and doing more drills, without a lunch. Food is getting scarce, and they're cutting back on our portions. Already some men in our regiment have gotten the fever again; they had to be sent out to the hospital by horseback to prevent more spreading.

Colonel Subir came by again today to tell us we would be moving out shortly. He had gotten word from General Rosecrans about the pursuit plan to drive the Rebels out of Chattanooga. I only know what I am writing, but I still don't know how a small town with only twenty-five hundred people in it can be so important. But for some reason it is. The Colonel said that General Rosecrans needs to receive a new shipment of maps of the Tennessee River and the forests near it before the pursuit, but we should be ready for battle at anytime. That's why we had to work so hard today—extra training. I personally plan to keep things going one day at a time. I learned that from Teddy.

I spoke of all the exhausting and disappointing events, now I'll speak of the fun ones. Teddy and I put on our own personal concert today, along with five other men; Walt, Jim, Shawn, Greg, and Andrew. Because I don't have too pretty a singing voice, I got to play Teddy's harmonica. When they were singing the church songs, I improvised mostly, but I got to play all five of the songs Teddy taught me. I also got to play solo on two songs I made up: "The Hard-Tac Song," and "The Boring Drill Song". The other soldiers who were watching loved it, they said I was a good musician, and Teddy had the most beautiful voice they'd ever heard. That I can honestly agree with.

Three days ago Teddy and I were talking over the fire. I told him that I was thinking of going back to school, if I pulled through the rest of the war. So we both agreed that I should get a college education no matter what. He made me promise that I would once I left the Union Army. I told Teddy that if the North won the war and all turned out for the best, he could come live with me. I know this made him feel happy because now he knows he has somewhere to go. I only hope I can say the same. But I feel that I'll be safe as long as I have him by my side.

After we made this pact a done deal, I told him that if the South won, I'd just purchase him no matter what the cost so that he could still live with me; I knew if we lost the war there would probably still be slavery, even in Northern border states like Maryland. But as for now I wish for the best for everybody. Even if all doesn't go exactly as planned, I will still always have faith.

Chapter Thirteen

When the lieutenant colonel's gun fired at four o'clock in the morning again on the third day of September, we all rushed out of our tents ready for another hard day of training. Instead of hearing him order us to line up for drill, we heard him shout the words we had been waiting so long to hear: "Gather your stuff men—we're moving out!"

A cold chill ran down my spine as I glanced towards Teddy's tent. He was peeping at mine at the same moment and our eyes met. We were all ready for this; we had been at the base for almost a full month. So he simply nodded his head at me in gratitude as I nodded back.

As more moments of silence passed, confusion between many of the men began to build up.

"Where are we moving to?"

"Which route are we going to take to get there?"

"How long will it take?"

"How many Rebels are there?"

"Who is going to lead us?" Questions were blurted out immediately as voices echoed.

"Silence, men!" Lieutenant Colonel Hurst shouted in frustration. All fell quiet as he continued. "We will be meeting with Colonel Subir and the rest of Cumberland five miles down-river. General Rosecrans will be there. From that point we will be crossing the river and pushing towards Chattanooga. That is the only information I can release until we meet up with the others. Now gather up your things quickly; we must arrive by sunrise." We all began to pack up.

When we arrived there just before six o'clock in the morning, we were tired and hungry. We had not yet had breakfast. However, we were also quite amazed at the number of troops that were there. It was much more than I had expected. When we met with General Rosecrans he said that there were even more soldiers and troops down the line and behind us. There were at least a few thousand where we were, listening to the general give his speech. He said that the whole Army of Cumberland was being split into four sections. Each section was going to cross at a different spot on the river; all far south of Chattanooga. He told us that eighteen-thousand troops were staying behind to guard our line of communications in central Tennessee.

After informing us of the plan, the general had a long, private discussion with Colonel Subir, probably mostly about where to cross along the Tennessee River. While this conversation was occurring, another colonel by the name of Frankson continued to keep us on our feet with practice drills. I looked around for Teddy but did not see him. There were too many men to see very far, but I knew I'd find him later.

In the afternoon of that same day, we met with yet another battalion of men, which added an additional five-thousand fresh faces. This particular battalion had a brigadier general who was going to guide all of us across the river. When it was all organized, General Rosecrans got on his horse and rode further south, probably going to another division.

At about three o'clock in the afternoon we arrived at the river and crossed over. It was difficult for the three colonels and the brigadier general to guide us all across in an orderly, organized manner. It all took over two hours, but they eventually pulled through. I still hadn't seen Teddy since we marched out of Fort Millgrow.

After we had all crossed and all obstacles were dodged, we marched eight more miles, out of sight of the river, before finally setting up camp. At about eight o'clock that night we were divided into our regiments for camp. We quickly set up our tents in regular arrangement. We were all eager to eat dinner, for we had had a late breakfast and no lunch. While my three tentmates and I were setting up our tent, I looked over and saw Teddy, Walt, Jim, and Shawn setting up theirs, three rows up and eight tents down.

"Teddy!" I called out with joy. I was quite happy that he appeared to be okay and still with the rest of us.

He turned around and raised his head toward me as he smiled and waved. "Hey, young'un!" he shouted. "Happy 17th birthday!"

I squinted my eyes in confusion. Did he just say it was my birthday? Was it my birthday? It took me a minute to recall, then I remembered: September 3rd, 1846. Sure enough, that was the day. How he knew that, to this day I could never figure out; I do not remember telling him. At the time, I almost questioned him, but something made me change my mind.

"Hey, Teddy," I called back.

"Yes, young'un?" he answered.

I wanted to ask him how he knew, my mouth even began to move, but no words came out. "Thanks," was all I could manage.

He shook his head with a smile, and he held up two fingers. "Still marching," he proudly responded.

"Yeah, still marching," I said as I held up two of my fingers.

After everyone had their tents set up, we were served cold beans and soup for dinner. I ate mine with Teddy by the fire, as we told each other more stories and spoke about events of the day. However, I did not stay there for very long, knowing full well that when dawn arrived again, it would be another long day of marching.

We awoke the next day at five o'clock in the morning. I was quite surprised they let us sleep in until our regular time. We were not rushed to get marching early in the morning like the day before. Instead, Brigadier General Hampton ordered us all to eat breakfast before we packed up. Later we found out that he had gotten word from General Rosecrans to slow down the pursuit for a day or two. I am still unsure of the reason for this.

After we had breakfast we were all lined up for a practice drill that lasted only an hour. It wasn't until after the drill that we began to pack up. After packing and cleaning we started the march north up to Chattanooga. We only marched 15 miles that day, half as much as I had expected. I was somewhat surprised that we only marched in a dozen different lines, considering that there were thousands of us. I saw Teddy once during the march, but I didn't get to talk to him until that night.

The next morning was the same marching routine, except we had to wake up at four o'clock. I had lost track of what day of the week it was. I think the commanding officers must have, too, because they didn't pay any attention to getting a break on Sundays anymore. We ate our breakfast quick, and packed up even quicker. We marched 20 miles north that day. I could smell another battle coming on when we got to Chattanooga. I thought I would become afraid at the thought of taking part in another battle, but I was not. That was partly because we had been preparing for this particular battle for so long, but it was mainly because of Teddy being there. Although we were not together every hour, I knew that whatever happened, he would still be marching right beside me.

Chapter Fourteen

Private Daniel Samsford, 3rd Regiment, 2nd Division,
in the Army of Cumberland

September 5th, 1863

Two days ago we left Fort Millgrow and crossed the Tennessee River far south of the city of Chattanooga. We've been put together with thousands of other men to form a large division of the Cumberland Army. I just got back from Teddy's tent. It isn't that cold tonight, but we set up a fire anyway. While we're on the march I mostly only get to talk to Teddy at night, but we both still make the most of the time we do have together.

I know that we're going to be in battle again soon. I continue to pray that all will turn out for the best. I trust the leader of our division, Brigadier General Joseph J. Hampton; he appears to be a decent man.

When Teddy and I were socializing around the fire he told me that he was just plain lucky for surviving Port Hudson. He said he wasn't sure if he could ever be that lucky again. I could tell that he felt some fear at the thought of being in another battle when he would be the only one who wasn't killing anybody. I knew that he felt left out in some ways, but still he would not go against his principles.

I made another agreement with Teddy. We both promised to not kill anyone and to protect each other. I am quite surprised that I made such a commitment, but I know it is for a good cause. He and I both know now that we'll be safe.

One thing I'm not so sure about is being in a division with so many other men. I have never marched with so many other troops before, not even at Gettysburg. We are still divided into our regiments at night and Lieutenant Colonel Hurst is still in full charge of ours, so it doesn't worry me too much. Also, General Rosecrans talked to us two days ago, and he seems to have the whole pursuit planned out pretty well. I know he must have put us in these large numbers for a good reason.

The day we left Fort Millgrow and crossed the Tennessee River was September 3rd; my birthday. Teddy was the one who reminded me of that date. I had forgotten. But I still remember that day was also exactly two months after Billy's tragic death at Gettysburg. I know now that I will remember that date for both reasons.

Chapter Fifteen

While marching, it was difficult for me to look around and find Teddy. I sometimes worried about him; I was concerned about how some of the white soldiers may be harrassing him. I also worried about where he was and what he was thinking. In the four weeks that I had known him, he had become such a part of me and changed so much of me. He had told me so many times that I had become an amazingly large part of him. It was because of him that I had decided that I was no longer going to kill any more men, no matter what the situation. I felt confident that I was making the right decision, and that we would both keep all of the promises that we made to each other. Although we both worried about each other during the day, we would both always end up in the same spot in the evening.

When we finally arrived in Chattanooga on the evening of September 8th, we were all prepared for an overnight battle. I had pretended to fall behind so I could find Teddy as he marched by. It took a while for me to spot him, but when I did he let me simply slip in line so I was marching directly in front of him.

"How you doing, young'un?" he asked gently.

"I'm okay, how about you?" I responded quietly.

"Ready for whatever they give me," he answered.

"Me, too. Still marching?" I held up my middle and index finger.

Teddy gave a grin. "Yeah, still marching," he replied as he did the same with his fingers.

We marched on until Colonel Subir gave the command to halt. We were in Chattanooga. General Hampton ordered some of us to center ourselves near a dry creek. I crouched down next to Teddy. As I glanced to the left way off in the distance, I could see some Yankee soldiers from another division. I could also see a few officers on horseback. According to Lieutenant Colonel Hurst, there were thousands more troops both to the left and right of us.

All of the officers kept telling us to stay completely silent and to wait before firing. We all looked as far as our eyes could measure, but still saw no Confederate soldiers. We kept being told to have patience. So we waited an hour, and soon two, as the sky fell into night.

"I don't think they're coming," Teddy grasped my shoulder.

We should have been relieved that there was going to be no head-on night battle, but something didn't seem right. I knew that General Hampton would not let us camp here without hearing direct orders from General Rosecrans. I felt he was getting frustrated and ready to send us farther into the farmlands of Chattanooga.

I looked up to see where the brigadier general was and found him a few hundred yards away. He was on a hill behind the dry creek, speaking to a man on horseback who was wearing a very shiny uniform.

I tapped Teddy on the back. "Does that look like a messenger to you?" I asked.

"Yeah, it does," he responded.

"Do you know what's going on?" I wondered.

"I'm sure the General will tell us," said Teddy with confidence.

Sure enough, it was only a few moments later that I saw General Hampton riding down the hill on horseback. He told us that the man he was talking to was General Rosecrans's devoted messenger. He continued by saying that General Rosecrans had discovered that General

Braxton Bragg had moved all of his Confederate troops out and had abandoned Chattanooga that morning.

Most of the soldiers were angry that they had marched all of those miles for nothing. Teddy and I were satisfied that we did not have to witness another battle. General Hampton had received orders from General Rosecrans to keep us all near the creek for the night and march out early in the morning. He told us we had to destroy the Rebels or they would be coming back to destroy us with reinforcements. I knew that neither I nor Teddy were going to destroy anyone, but still we played along with it and tried to get some sleep. I had never slept in the bed of a creek before, but I knew that Teddy had slept in a trench for many nights at Port Hudson, which was probably even less comfortable.

The next morning we awoke at four o'clock and marched west out of Chattanooga and into a forested area. Teddy was marching out of sight from where I could see him. I still kept looking behind me to try to catch a glance at him, and at one moment I thought I did. I think he saw me, too. All together, we marched about 25 miles that day. We set up a regular camp in the forest when sundown arrived again. We didn't build a fire that night, but I still got to talk to Teddy for a little while.

The day after that was quite similar, except not as harsh. We didn't have to wake up until half past four, and we only marched 21 miles. Another messenger had spoken to General Hampton that day. He said that General Rosecrans had reason to believe that General Bragg had positioned his troops over in Georgia, somewhere near a road called Lafayette. He had a plan for us to march around them and come up from behind. In order to do this, our division had to be split in half, but none of the regiments were split apart. General Hampton rode his horse northeast, leading the half of our division that our regiment was not a part of. He ordered Colonel Subir to take charge of our half of the division. We marched in a northeastern direction. It seemed like a clever enough plan.

The next few days were, for the most part, the same. Messengers came around, we marched through forest and farmland, Colonel Subir thoroughly thought out the military strategy, and Teddy and I spoke kindly to each other at night. Our limited socializing time did not affect our relationship at all; we were still brothers.

Chapter Sixteen

Private Daniel Samsford, 3rd Regiment, 2nd Division,
1st Half, Army of Cumberland

September 14th, 1863

The past six days have been pretty much the same. Four days ago our division was split in half. Colonel Subir is in charge of our half; we're a bit smaller than the other half. On the eighth we reached Chattanooga and prepared for battle by spending over two hours huddled up in a dry creek bed. Then we were informed that General Bragg's Confederate troops abandoned Chattanooga earlier. We spent the whole night in that creek and left the next morning. I slept by Teddy where I knew I'd be safe.

Later we found out that General Bragg's whole army was dispersed on Lafayette Road, in Georgia, so that is where we're marching to. I hear that the rest of Cumberland is quite scattered, and most are marching back towards Chattanooga to claim it when we drive the Rebels out. As for us, we're marching to a place called Chickamauga; so far it's been a very long march. When we arrive, we're going to come up behind the Confederate army on Lafayette Road—that's the plan. Teddy and I are still holding true to the promises we made to each other.

I heard Bragg's army has already made two attempts to destroy ours, failing both times. There has been no battle yet, but I know that soon there will be. I doubt it will be in Chattanooga as originally planned. If I had a guess, I would say that it will be in Georgia, maybe near Lafayette Road. But we will not know anything until it happens.

Colonel Subir says that we will be receiving reinforcement troops soon. He says that General George Thomas's 14th Corp and General Alexander McCook's 20th Corp are marching in, but it's supposed to be a secret. He says that will build up our army to around sixty-two thousand. He also says that the Rebels may already have reinforcements, too, so we should be ready for anything. They have told us to be ready for so long, maybe this time there will actually be something for us to be ready for.

Teddy and I still have the most socializing time at night. Yesterday night we decided that if I do make it back home, the college I will be going to will still be the University of Maryland. Once again, I made a loyal promise to him.

Chapter Seventeen

On the morning of September 18th, we awoke at four o'clock, ready for the pursuit towards Lafayette Road. I was quite unaware that this was a day that would change my life forever. We began our march. I tried to stay with Teddy the whole way. Everyone was feeling very confident and thought that we were surely ready for battle. I can honestly say that I was getting pretty tired of marching all around, so I would be glad when it was finally over.

I only wished that there didn't have to be another battle to end it all. But perhaps there didn't. Maybe General Bragg and the Confederates would retreat completely and forget about Chattanooga. We had thousands of Yankee troops in the town as it was. They would have to drive us out to take control of it again. Maybe they didn't want to go through all of that trouble. It was a nice thought, but I didn't find it very likely.

What I did not know was that very same morning that we were marching into Chickamauga heading towards Lafayette Road, General

Bragg ordered his army to drive our army out of Chattanooga. Not even General Rosecrans knew of this plan.

While the Rebels were marching out, we were marching in, in the same direction. After marching about 15 miles and having two practice drills, it was already one o'clock in the afternoon. We then took a midday lunch break about four miles south of Jay's Mill, which was a small forest we planned to cut through in order to get to Lafayette Road.

After the lunch break, we began marching again and arrived at Jay's Mill at around three o'clock in the afternoon. I was still right by Teddy. The inside of Jay's Mill was a thick woodland, so we all spread out slightly. At the shadowy area with more trees, Teddy and I spread apart about 50 feet. At one of these dark spots as I was maneuvering around the trees, our whole regiment and others in our division saw a sight that made us all freeze in terror. The Rebel army was directly in front of us, marching in our direction.

I gulped for air as I felt myself shiver. When they saw us, they too froze in silence. We had been preparing for this battle for almost two months, but none of us were ready for a collision like this. It was their general who first yelled: "Men, fire at will!"

Most of the Union soldiers soon caught on and began to fire as well. Because I had made a promise not to kill, I began to look all around me for a place to hide, and for Teddy.

"Teddy, where are you?!" I bellowed out as I watched men fall all around me. "Teddy, please!" I heard only gunfire for several more minutes as I blockaded myself behind a tree.

"Daniel!" I finally heard a soothing voice call out. "Daniel, over here!"

I looked southeast of where I was standing; hundreds of yards in the distance I saw Teddy standing by what looked like a small, deep hole in the ground. "Teddy!" I called out with relief, I was quite thankful that he appeared to be okay. I began to run towards him with eagerness, I did not look behind me at all of the dying men. I knew there was nothing that I could do to help any of them.

Within the first one-hundred yards of running, I was stopped dead in my tracks. A sharp burst of pain erupted just above my right elbow. I shouted in agony as I glanced toward my open wound. A bullet had struck the upper part of my arm; blood was gushing out rapidly.

"Daniel!" I heard Teddy shout. As quick as lightening, he picked me up and carried me to the open hole, which appeared to be a dry well. He removed his undershirt and wrapped it around my bleeding wound. He put his blue Yankee overcoat on top of mine to keep me warm. He was bare-chested and the dozens of large gashes and scars from previous whippings on his back were now visible, but everyone else was too busy shooting their rifles and muskets to even notice.

The next thing that I remember was waking up with a white sheet on top of me that was drenched in my blood. I was lying on a wooden bed frame with a thin mattress in a large tent. There were men moaning in agony all around me; most were on the ground as there didn't appear to be enough beds for everyone. Some of the men were missing limbs, and some were as pale as ghosts.

I felt a warm washcloth wet my forehead as my eyes came into focus. There I saw a beautiful, dark-haired woman with bright green eyes. She appeared very worn-out although she probably wasn't any older than 30.

"Mom?" I mumbled deliriously, still unsure of where I was.

"No dear," she responded. "I'm just a nurse." She then scooped up the dirty washcloth and bucket and started to wet the head of the man in bed next to me.

I turned my head away from her and saw Teddy sitting on the grass staring at the words in his Bible. It was then that I remembered that I had been shot. "Teddy?" I murmured.

He set the Bible down and looked up at me with a closed-mouth smile. "Hey, young'un," he said softly. "How you feeling?"

"Okay," I answered. "Where are we?"

"We're at the Yankee Medical Hospital in Hillpoint, Georgia, about 12 miles south and east of Jay's Mill."

"You carried me that far?" I questioned.

Teddy looked toward the ground. "Well, yeah," he answered. "You would have died if I hadn't, plus I have to keep my muscles strong somehow."

"How's the battle going?" I asked. My throat was very dry.

Teddy soon sensed this and poured me the remaining water from his canteen. "I'm not sure," he replied. "You've been out for over 18 hours, you know. To be honest I'd say that it ain't going too well for either side. A collision of troops ain't a good way to start. Last I heard the generals keep sending in more reinforcements. We're both damn lucky we got out alive."

"You saved my life again, Teddy, and you stayed with me the whole time. Thank you."

After hearing me speak those words, Teddy's face filled with sorrow. "Ah young'un, I know you would have done the same thing for me," he said.

I placed my head on the sheet as I wondered if I would have done the same thing for him; I hoped so.

Teddy's somber face began to choke up, and I knew that something must have been wrong. "When I finally got you here, they gave you a big shot of whisky," he said.

I knew exactly what he was getting at. Since I'd woken up, I had not used nor looked at my wounded right arm. I quickly and painfully sprang up in the bed and saw that it was no longer there. My shirt was off and the remaining stub that ended between my shoulder and elbow was tightly wrapped in thin cloth and had very little circulation.

"Ahhhhhhhh! My God!" I screamed with fear and disgust.

"Shhhh, Daniel, Daniel," he whispered. "They had to cut it off; you would have died if they hadn't," he attempted to calm me.

"You let them cut off my arm?" I questioned my best friend.

"Daniel, the bullet went straight through your arm, if they didn't cut it off, it would have rotted off," he gently informed me. I continued to breathe heavily. "Please understand that it was for the best, Daniel. There was nothing more that could have been done. Do you understand?" He asked.

I was still breathing heavily as seconds and soon minutes passed. My breathing soon quieted but it was still difficult to concentrate when so many others were in pain around me. "I don't completely understand, but over time I'll try," I said as I laid my head down again. The remaining portion of my right arm was completely numb.

"Thank you, Daniel, for remaining strong," said Teddy.

"Thank you for teaching me to live without regret," I responded.

A few moments passed before he spoke again. "Well, now that I know that you're okay, I must be getting back to the battlefield." He got to his feet.

I was shocked. Why did he want to go back if he wasn't going to take part, and he could stay here with me? "No!" I bellowed. "Please don't leave me here alone!"

Teddy looked down at me. "I have to, young'un," he said. "One of the officers will come by and make me, and maybe shoot me if I don't. I ain't wounded like you."

"Please don't go until they come and take you away, I need you to stay here with me Teddy," I willingly released tears from my eyes. "This time I'm telling you it's for the best," I said.

Teddy walked around my mattress and grasped my left hand with kindness. "I'm sorry, Daniel," he spoke in seriousness. "It's my duty as a soldier for the Union to be in a battle when necessary, even if I don't fight. I promise that I'll be okay no matter what happens. As long as I have my Bible with me, I know I'll be just fine." He placed his Holy Bible over the bloodstained sheets.

I removed my surviving hand from his grasp to wipe the falling tears from my face. I held the Bible near my tear-filled eyes as I read its words to Teddy Blocodle one last time. I began with the page that it was on: "1 Samuel, Chapter 17: The Story of David and Goliath ..."

Teddy listened intently, for the final time.

After I was done reading the story, Teddy gave me his harmonica and told me to take good care of it. He said that it may not be in this lifetime, but eventually he would come back for it. He also told me that when I was unconscious he overheard some officers talking to each other. They said that nearly the entire 3rd regiment of Cumberland had been killed in the first three hours of battle.

"It was you, young'un, who likely saved my life," said Teddy. "You sacrificed your arm so that I could live to see another sunrise and spend another day with my best friend."

"Okay, so I suppose now we're even," I wept.

Teddy left behind what remained of his ammunition, but took his rifle with him. "Don't forget about me, little brother," he said with compassion.

"I won't forget about you, big brother," I was now bawling. I wrapped my remaining arm around him as we hugged for the last time. "I won't forget about our promises either; I swear I won't," I assured him.

"I trust you," he replied simply. "And don't forget that I'll always be with you in your heart." He began to cry also.

I moved my face from his torn overcoat and spoke to him the only words of wisdom that I knew to say at that time. "Teddy, I'd shed a million tears to keep you alive. That's what true brothers do."

Hearing this, Teddy's face remained expressionless as many tears fell from his eyes. "The same to you, Daniel Samsford," he bellowed out. "The hidden tears will always still be marching."

I held up my middle and index fingers next to his. "Still marching," I said with empathy.

"Goodbye, young'un." His caring voice echoed through my heart. Then he turned around and quickly marched out of sight.

The next day, after I had received more much needed rest, Walt and Jim limped into the makeshift hospital tent, both with shrapnel wounds in their legs from an explosion. It was the two of them who broke the news to me. Teddy had made it back to the battlefield, and had died a hero. He had pushed the two of them out of the direct line of fire so that their injuries were only minor in comparison to his. Shrapnel had pierced a hole in his chest. Shawn wanted to carry him to safety, but he died instantly. I was deeply saddened to hear the news, but not entirely surprised. I had prayed for the best, but knew that in times of war, outcomes are all too often extremely disappointing. Yet I still play the harmonica that he gave me from time to time and remember warmly the strong friendship that we shared.

A few hours after Walt and Jim came to the hospital to have their wounds treated and share the bad news with me, Shawn appeared without injury to check on us and let us know that he was the only one in our regiment that he knew of who had escaped without injury or death. Worse, the battle was not yet over. However, he did tell me that Teddy's broken body, held together now primarily by his blue Union uniform, still carried his bloodstained Bible. Walt, Jim and Shawn all promised me then that when they returned to the battlefield to bury the dead, they would be sure to give full honor to Teddy, and would make sure he was buried with his Bible in his pocket.

I regret having missed his informal memorial service due to having to recover from my own injuries, and now having to learn to write with my left hand. I had watched him leave to go defend our country without violence before losing yet another brother forever. But I knew that I would remain determined to accept reality because of that man, my second brother, the spirits of both of my late brothers would remain in my heart forever, and in life, I would march on.

Three days after the battle of Chickamauga was won by the Confederacy on the 23rd of September in the year 1863, I was transported to the nearest railroad station by horseback. From there I got the privilege of riding on my first train, all the way up to McSherville, Maryland. The rest of the surviving Union Army of Cumberland was trapped in Chattanooga by the Confederates. With more reinforcements, the Union fought and won the battle of Chattanooga, finally taking full control of the city on the 25th of November. But the war didn't end for 16 ½ long months after that.

I graduated from the University of Maryland in 1868. I was still given the complete four-year scholarship. I became a professor of history and literature, and a well-known writer. In the summer of 1873, I married and later had four beautiful children. We named my oldest after my father who died in a farming accident only 15 days before he was born. My second and only daughter we named after my late mother. The third child we named after my brother, William Joseph Samsford, and my youngest, after my other brother: Theodore James Blocodle.

Over six-hundred and twenty-thousand men died in that war. Over four-hundred thousand more were wounded. I was one of them. Over thirty-four thousand died in the battle of Chickamauga alone. But I'll always remember one; I'll always remember how he saved my life, twice. I'll always remember how he changed so many things about me for the better, how he brought miracles into my life. I'll always remember how he helped me face the truth, and I'll always remember how he lived one day longer because of me.

16/P
9 780881 441161